JUST·FOR·ME™

HUNGRY BEAR

Written by Rosalyn Rosenbluth
Illustrated by Jo-Ellen Bosson

Modern Publishing
A Division of Unisystems, Inc.
New York, New York 10022

Hungry Bear is having lunch—
four peanut butter and jelly
sandwiches, two apples, one
cupcake, and a very big thermos
bottle filled with milk.

"You eat entirely too much," says
Proud Peacock, pecking daintily at a
seed.

Hungry Bear frowns. "I'm hungry,"
he says as he turns his back.

Proud Peacock walks around so Hungry Bear can see him. He stretches his neck, spreads his beautiful feathers and asks Hungry Bear, "How do you expect to have a trim figure like mine if you keep eating like a pig?"

Hungry Bear frowns even more. "I'm not a pig," he says. He takes a bite of his sandwich and growls a little.

"Leave Hungry Bear alone," says Gentle Lamb as she nibbles on a blade of grass. "He's hungry." But even she cannot help staring as all the sandwiches disappear down Hungry Bear's throat.

"Well, it's for his own good," says Proud Peacock. "Wouldn't you rather be lean and handsome like me?" he asks Hungry Bear.

Hungry Bear watches Proud Peacock. He thinks for a moment. "Maybe I'll try dieting for a few days. Well, maybe just tomorrow."

The next day Hungry Bear brings his lunchbox to the clearing and opens it, but he does not eat. He sits playing his little banjo, sighing and staring at the sandwiches.

"Your mother certainly packs a nice lunch," says Gentle Lamb.

Hungry Bear growls and Gentle Lamb backs away a little.

"You must be very hungry," says Gentle Lamb. Hungry Bear growls a little louder.

"You're doing wonderfully well," says Proud Peacock. "You will be the best-looking bear in the forest."

Just then Slow Turtle arrives at the clearing. He looks at Hungry Bear's lunchbox. "Why aren't you eating, Hungry Bear?" he asks. "Are you sick?"

"He's dieting. He wants to look beautiful like me," answers Proud Peacock.

"He's giving his poor stomach a rest," says Gentle Lamb.

"You are both silly," Slow Turtle says to Gentle Lamb and Proud Peacock. "And you are silliest of all," he says to Hungry Bear. "You must eat as much as you can now because you will sleep all through the winter and not eat anything at all."

"Not anything?" says Gentle Lamb. "Oh, poor Hungry Bear."

"Well, how was I supposed to know that?" says Proud Peacock as he tiptoes away.

Hungry Bear smiles. "No wonder I'm so hungry," he shouts as he grabs his lunchbox and gobbles everything up in four large gulps.

But the next day, when Hungry Bear comes to the clearing with his lunch, his friends are not there. "I hate to eat alone," he says.

Suddenly, Proud Peacock, Gentle Lamb, and Slow Turtle jump out from behind the bushes.

"Surprise!" they shout as they offer Hungry Bear a big bowl of honey and berries.

"Eat all you want, Hungry Bear!" says Gentle Lamb.

"Even if it makes you fatter," says Proud Peacock.

"It's good for you," says Slow Turtle.

Hungry Bear is very happy. "Now you're talking," he says. And he picks up the bowl and starts to eat.